A NOTE TO PARENTS

Disney's **First Readers Level 1** books were developed with the beginning reader in mind. They feature large, easy-to-read type, lots of repetition, and simple vocabulary.

One of the most important ways parents can help their child develop a love of reading is by providing an *environment* of reading. Every time you discuss a book, read aloud to your child, or your child observes you reading, you promote the development of early reading skills and habits. Here are some tips to help you use **Disney's First Readers Level 1** books with your child:

★ Tell the story about the original Disney film or video. Storytelling is crucial to language development. A young child needs a language *foundation* before reading skills can begin to emerge.

★ Talk about the illustrations in the book. Beginning readers need to use illustrations to gather clues about unknown words or to understand the story.

★ Read aloud to your child. When you read aloud, smoothly run your finger under the text. Do not stop at each word. Enliven the text for your child by using a different voice for each character. In other words, be an actor—and have fun!

★ "Read it again!" Children love hearing stories read again and again. When they begin reading on their own, repetition helps them feel successful. Maintain patience, be encouraging, and expect to read the same books over and over.

★ Play "question and answer." Use the After-Reading Fun activities provided at the end of each book to further enhance your child's learning process.

Remember that early-reading experiences that you share with your child can help him or her to become a confident and successful reader later on!

— Patricia Koppman
Past President
International Reading Association

Based on the Pooh Stories by A.A. Milne (copyright The Pooh Properties Trust).

First Edition published by Disney Press, New York, NY
This edition published by Grolier Books, ISBN: 0-7172-6477-7
Grolier Books is a division of Grolier Enterprises, Inc.

Pooh's Scavenger Hunt

by Isabel Gaines
Illustrated by Studio Orlando

Disney's First Readers — Level 1

GROLIER
B O O K S
BOOK CLUB EDITION

Pooh and his friends
meet Christopher Robin.

They want to play
a game.

Christopher Robin says
they should have a
scavenger hunt.

Tigger has never heard
of that game.

But Christopher Robin
says it is fun.

He thinks of things
they can look for.

He tells them
to look for . . .

a purple flower,

a small jar
of honey,

and a red leaf.

So Pooh and his
friends start to look.

They go to Pooh's
house first.

Pooh finds a small
jar of honey.

They all help Pooh get
the jar down. Oops!

Next they look for
a leaf and a flower.

But Pooh forgets
their colors.

Kanga finds a
red flower instead.

Roo finds a yellow leaf!
But it is not red.

Now they want to
show Christopher Robin.

Christopher Robin is
sitting on a stump.

They tell him they
found three things.

Christopher Robin says
they really found four.

What is the fourth?

They found that friends have fun working together!

Enhance the reading experience with follow-up questions to help your child develop reading comprehension and increase his/her awareness of words.

Approach this with a sense of play. Make a game of having your child answer the questions. You do not need to ask all the questions at one time. Let these questions be fun discussions rather than a test. If your child doesn't have instant recall, encourage him/her to look back into the book to "research" the answers. You'll be modeling what good readers do and, at the same time, forging a sharing bond with your child.

Pooh's Scavenger Hunt

1. What game did Pooh and his friends play?

2. Where was the honey jar found?

3. Did Pooh and his friends find the right flower?

4. Hunt for words with double letters in the story.

5. Who are the characters in the story?

6. What's your favorite game? How do you play it?

Answers: 1. scavenger hunt. 2. in Pooh's house. 3. no, they found a red flower. 4. *possible answers:* meet, tell, yellow, Pooh, look, sitting, all, Tigger, small, three. 5. Christopher Robin, Pooh, Tigger, Rabbit, Eeyore, Roo, Kanga, Owl, and Piglet. 6. answers will vary.